For Esther.

I promised you a puppy, and you're still waiting. I'm sorry!

Will you accept this book instead? —J.L.

For Eunice,

my wonderful agent —M.A.

Published by Roaring Brook Press

Roaring Brook Press is a division of Holtzbrinck Publishing Holdings Limited Partnership

120 Broadway, New York, NY 10271 • mackids.com

Library of Congress Cataloging-in-Publication Data is available.

Originally published in Great Britain in 2022 by Andersen Press Ltd.

First American edition, 2022

Printed in China by RR Donnelley Asia Printing Solutions Ltd., Dongguan City, Guangdong Province

ISBN 978-1-250-83415-7 (hardcover)

1 3 5 7 9 10 8 6 4 2

The Pet Potato

written by
Josh Lacey

illustrated by
Momoko Abe

Roaring Brook Press
New York

All Albert wanted was a pet.
But his mom and dad always said no.

They said, "We're too busy for a dog."

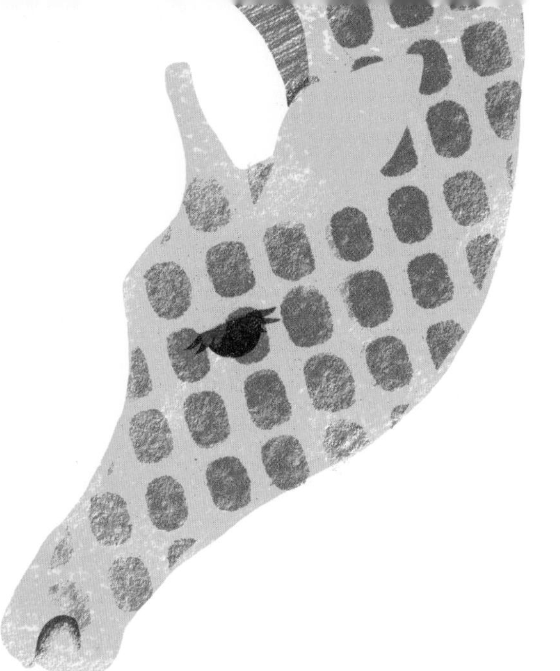

They said, "Cats make
Mom sneeze."

They said, "Rabbits need
a big garden."

They said, "Of course we can't have a giraffe!
Don't be silly."

Albert never gave up. There was nothing else he wanted for Christmas or his birthday.

Morning and evening,

he begged his parents for a pet.

Until one day, Dad called him over and said, "I have a present for you."

It was a small package wrapped up in blue paper and tied with ribbon.

"What's this?" Albert asked. "There's only one way to find out," Dad said.

Albert opened
the package and
inside he found

a potato.

"You wanted a pet," Dad said. "There you go."
"That is not a pet," Albert said. "That is a potato."
"It's a pet potato," Dad said.

Dad made jokes like that all the time. Albert had learned to ignore them. He put the potato away and forgot about it.

Potatoes can't look sad.

Or lonely.

But somehow this one did.

The next day, Albert laid out his train tracks.

When he had finished, the potato
went for a ride in one of the cars.

Albert built a tower with a room at the top.
From there the potato could see for miles around.

Albert took the potato to the playground.

It swung on the swings

and rolled down the slide

and went

round and

round and

round on the merry-go-round.

Mickey wanted to use the potato as a soccer ball, but Albert said no. That wouldn't be nice.

Potatoes aren't allowed in swimming pools, so it had to stay with Mom while Albert had his lesson.

When they went to the library, Albert and the potato took turns choosing.

For some reason, the potato particularly liked books about pirates.

When Albert took a bath, the potato sat on the edge of the tub.

After bath time, it listened to his stories.

And every night,
the potato slept
on Albert's pillow.

Then one morning, the potato disappeared.

Albert searched his room, but it was nowhere to be seen.

It wasn't playing with the trains.
Or up in the tower.
It might have gone for a walk.
Or down to the store to buy some milk.

But potatoes can't really do that.
Can they?

Albert found his potato in the trash. "Put it back, please," Mom said. Albert refused. "You can't throw him away!"

"I'm sorry, Albert, but it's smelly and moldy," Mom said. "It's going bad. I don't want that thing in my house."

Dad dug a hole.
Albert put his potato
in the ground.

They covered him up.

They said goodbye.

Mom and Dad sat down with Albert for a serious talk.
"You were so good at looking after the potato," Mom said. "We think you're ready for a real pet."

Dad said, "We're going to get you a hamster."

But Albert didn't want a hamster.
Nor did he want a dog, a cat, a rabbit, or even a giraffe.
He wanted his own pet back.
His beautiful, perfect pet.

To Albert's surprise, after a couple of weeks, a little shoot appeared.

The shoot grew leaves.

Dad gave a pitchfork to Albert.

Every day, the leaves were bigger.

Albert dug and dug until he found all the potatoes.

There were enough for everyone.